The H. A. REY
TREASURY OF STORIES

H. A. Rey and Margret Rey

DOVER PUBLICATIONS, INC
MINEOLA, NEW YORK

D1227786

Bibliographical Note

The H. A. Rey Treasury of Stories, first published by Dover Publications, Inc., in 2015, is a republication of the following works: *Tit for Tat* (Harper & Brothers Publishers, New York and London, 1942); *Elizabite: Adventures of a Carnivorous Plant* (Houghton Mifflin Company, Boston, 1942); *Billy's Picture* (Houghton Mifflin Company, Boston, 1948); and *Zebrology* (Chatto & Windus, London, 1937).

Library of Congress Cataloging-in-Publication Data

Rey, H. A. (Hans Augusto), 1898–1977, author.
    [Short stories. Selections]
    The H.A. Rey treasury of stories / H. A. Rey, Margret Rey.
       p. cm.
    The H. A. Rey Treasury of Stories, first published by Dover Publications, Inc., in 2015, is a republication of the following works: *Tit for Tat* (Harper & Brothers Publishers, New York and London, 1942); *Elizabite: Adventures of a Carnivorous Plant* (Houghton Mifflin Company, Boston, 1942); *Billy's Picture* (Houghton Mifflin Company, Boston, 1948); and *Zebrology* (Chatto & Windus, London, 1937)."
      Summary: Four stories from the creators of Curious George present a place where human and animal roles are reversed, the antics of a hungry plant in a botanist's laboratory, Billy the Bunny's attempts to paint a picture, and a wordless celebration of the common ground that lies beneath appearances.
    Includes bibliographical note.
    ISBN-13: 978-0-486-78468-7 (paperback)
    ISBN-10: 0-486-78468-1
    1. Children's stories, American. [1. Stories in rhyme. 2. Stories without words. 3. Animals—Fiction. 4. Carnivorous plants—Fiction. 5. Short stories.] I. Rey, Margret, author. II. Title. III. Title: Treasury of stories.

PZ8.3.R32Hae 2015
[E]—dc23

           2014041165

Manufactured in the United States by Courier Corporation
78468101   2015
www.doverpublications.com

CONTENTS

TIT for TAT

by

H.A. REY

Matt and his little turtle
   Lived right here in this town.
   Matt used to tease the turtle
   And turn it upside down.

The turtle begged: "O stop it, please!"
But that was all in vain:
It tried so hard but could not get
Back on its feet again.

Matt's uncle, Angus Appleface,
Said: "Matt, you should not do
To others anything you don't
Want them to do to you.

"Pretend that things were turned around
And fancy you would lie
In such a shell flat on your back—
Imagine how you'd cry!"

"Gee, Uncle, you are right!" said Matt.
"Well, if you want to know
What I found out," said Appleface,
"Come to my studio.

"I have a great invention there,
A TURN-A-VISION SET.
Just turn a switch and light the screen
And this is what you get:

"You first see all the things WE do
To animals, and then
You see the very same things done
By animals to men."

The show is on!—The HORSE must draw
The buggy down the street.
The coachman holds the reins and looks
Severely from his seat.

Now move the turn-a-vision switch
And you'll see clearly that
The story has been turned around:
The HORSE plays TIT for TAT.

The fisherman sits on the bridge.
He's busy catching FISH.
He puts them in his pail and thinks:
They'll make a lovely dish!

Now move the turn-a-vision switch
And you'll see clearly that
The story has been turned around:
The FISH plays TIT for TAT.

The shepherd shears the little SHEEP:
He puts them on his knees
And cuts away their curly wool.
The sheep feel cold, and sneeze.

Now move the turn-a-vision switch
And you'll see clearly that
The story has been turned around:
The SHEEP play TIT for TAT.

A piece of cake is in the trap.
The trap is on the floor.
The MOUSE that comes to try the cake
Can get away no more.

Now move the turn-a-vision switch
And you'll see clearly that
The story has been turned around:
The MICE play TIT for TAT.

The **COWS** start running when they see
The cowboys with their lasso.
They moo and think: why don't they let
Us eat in peace our grass, oh!

Now move the turn-a-vision switch
And you'll see clearly that
The story has been turned around:
The COW plays TIT for TAT.

This man here likes CANARY birds
Because their song is sweet.
He always keeps them in a cage
And feeds them shredded wheat.

Now move the turn-a-vision switch
And you'll see clearly that
The story has been turned around:
The BIRDS play TIT for TAT.

DOGS in the cities have no luck,
For when they meet each other
Their hurried owners will not even
Let them greet each other.

Now move the turn-a-vision switch
And you'll see clearly that
The story has been turned around:
the DOGS play TIT for TAT.

The lady looks into the glass
With a contented air:
What lovely things those FOXES are
Around the neck to wear!

Now move the turn-a-vision switch
And you'll see clearly that
The story has been turned around:
The FOX plays TIT for TAT.

To carry babies into homes
Is quite a heavy strain.
The STORK must do it every day
In sunshine, snow or rain.

Now move the turn-a-vision switch
And you'll see clearly that
The story has been turned around:
The STORK plays TIT for TAT.

"My friends," said Uncle Appleface,
"The show is now complete!"
Matt and the turtle clapped their hands
And Matt cried: "What a treat!"

And then the turtle heartily
Shook the Professor's hand
And said, "I thank you very much,
I also think it's grand!

"Of course, most of us animals
Are patient and will thus
Not *really* think of paying back
What people do to us.

"But all the children far and wide
Should go and see this show
For they will see how *others* feel
And then be kind, I know.

"And from now on I'm sure that Matt
Will be a thoughtful friend
And no more turn me upside down!"
       This is the happy end.

ELIZABITE

ADVENTURES OF
A CARNIVOROUS PLANT

by

H. A. REY

TO

PEGGY

YOU would not think that plants like meat.
Well, some plants do. They catch and eat
Small insects, such as flies and ants,
And they are called

CARNIVOROUS PLANTS.

One of them came to world-wide fame;
ELIZABITE, that was her name.

Elizabite smiles at the sky
While a mosquito passes by.

Right in the middle of its flight
She captures it with great delight.

Elizabite smiles at the sky . . .
There comes another passer-by.

It's Doctor White, a scientist,
And well-known as a botanist.

"This plant is very rare indeed!
I'll take her home and get the seed."

"She's caught me——Ouch!" cries Doctor White,
"I did not know this plant could bite."

He now tries out a safer way,
And he succeeds without delay.

Victorious he leaves the place,
A smile of triumph on his face.

Here in the doctor's laboratory
Continues the amazing story.

The plant, for once, behaves all right.
She gets a drink from Doctor White,

And even, as a special treat,
Frankfurters, for she's fond of meat.

But Scotty thinks with jealousy,
Frankfurters should belong to ME!

Alas, it never pays to steal!
Elizabite will spoil his meal.

A sudden snap—a cry—a wail—
And there goes Scotty minus tail!

Mary, the maid, comes with her broom
To tidy up the messy room.

And, unsuspecting, turns her back:
A tempting aim for an attack!

Elizabite's bad deeds require
A solid fence of strong barbed wire.

And Doctor White reports the case
Now to Professor Appleface.

But Appleface declares, "I doubt it
Till I myself find out about it."

He soon obtains the evidence
Despite the new barbed wire fence.

"We have to keep Elizabite
Chained to the kennel now," says White.

This burglar does not realize

The danger of his enterprise . . .

Next morning White perceives with fright
Someone inside Elizabite!

"How brave of her to catch this man!
Let's put him in the prison van."

Of course, Elizabite can't stay
With White. She now is on her way

To a new home, the nearby Zoo.

Here she became—and this is true—

At once the most outstanding sight.
Surrounded by her children bright
She lived in happiness and glory
Up to this day...

Here ends the story.

Billy's Picture

by

Margret & H. A. Rey

"I want to draw a picture,"
said Billy the Bunny.

So he took a pencil and began to draw.
Just then Penny the Puppy happened to
come along.

"That's a pretty picture," said Penny.
"But it needs a HEAD. Please let me do it."
And he took the pencil and drew a head with
long floppy ears just like his own.

"There you are," he said. "That's the way it should be." "But. . . ." Billy began. Just then Greta the Goose happened to come along.

"That's a lovely picture," said Greta.
"But it needs FEET. Please let me do them."
And she took the pencil and drew a pair of
feet just like her own.

"There you are," she said. "That's the way it should be." "But what. . . ." Billy began. Just then Paul the Porcupine happened to come along.

"That's a wonderful picture," said Paul. "But it needs QUILLS. Please let me do them." And he took the pencil and drew lots and lots of quills just like his own.

"There you are," he said. "That's the way
it should be." "But what I. . . ." Billy began.
Just then Ronny the Rooster happened to
come along.

"That's a beautiful picture," said Ronny. "But it needs a COMB. Please let me do it." And he took the pencil and drew a comb just like his own.

"There you are," he said. "That's the way it should be." "But what I wanted. . . ." Billy began. Just then Oliver the Owl happened to come along.

"That's a great picture," said Oliver. "But it needs WINGS. Please let me do them." And he took the pencil and drew a pair of wings just like his own.

"There you are," he said. "That's the way it should be." "But what I wanted to. . . ." Billy began. Just then Maggie the Mouse happened to come along.

"That's a sweet picture," said Maggie.
"But it needs a TAIL. Please let me do it."
And she took the pencil and drew a tail just
like her own.

"There you are," she said. "That's the
way it should be." "But what I wanted to
draw...." Billy began.

Just then Eric the Elephant happened to come along. "That's a delightful picture," said Eric. "But it needs a TRUNK. Please let me do it."

**And he took the pencil and drew a trunk
just like his own. "There you are," he said.
"That's the way it should be."**

"But what I wanted to draw." Billy began once more —and this time nobody happened to come along—"what I wanted to draw isn't a PUPPYGOOSE or a PORCUPHANT or whatever you call this silly picture. All I wanted to draw was a picture of myself!"

Here Billy began to cry and for a moment nobody said anything. Then everybody started to talk at the same time.

"A picture of myself—that's just what I wanted to do!" said Penny and Greta and Paul and Ronny and Oliver and Eric.

Billy stopped crying. "Why not do it then?" he said.

And that's what they did: Eric drew an
elephant and Maggie drew a mouse. Paul
drew a porcupine and Greta drew a goose.

Penny drew a puppy and Oliver drew an owl. Ronny drew a rooster—and can you guess what Billy drew?

That's what he drew!

H. A. REY

ZEBROLOGY